the OHIO experience

CAROLE MARSH

Published by
GALLOPADE INTERNATIONAL
Peachtree City • Georgia

The Ohio Experience™

CEO & EDITOR	Carole Marsh
PUBLISHER	Michael Longmeyer
CONSULTING EDITOR	Michele Yother
PROJECT DIRECTOR	Sherry Moss
CONTRIBUTING WRITERS	Carole Marsh, Chad Beard, Rachel Moss
COPY EDITOR	Chad Beard
DESIGN	Michele Winkelman
EDITORIAL ASSISTANT	Rachel Moss

Gallopade is proud to be a member of the National Council for Social Studies, as well as these educational organizations and associations:

OCSS • NCSS • NSSEA • NMGC • International Reading Association • ASCD

GALLOPADE INTERNATIONAL
665 Highway 74 South
Suite 600
Peachtree City, GA 30269
(800) 536-2438
(800) 871-2979 (fax)

Find us on the World Wide Web at:
www.gallopade.com

Copyright © 2004 by Carole Marsh

NOTICE OF RIGHTS
All Rights Reserved. No part of this publication may be reproduced in whole or in part, stored in a retrieval system, or transmitted in any form or by any means, electronic, mechanical, photocopying, recording or otherwise, without written permission from the publisher. For information, contact Gallopade International.

Original illustrations and art by:
Cecil Anderson, Lucyna A. M. Green, and Michele Winkelman

The Ohio Experience is a trademark of Carole Marsh and Gallopade International, Inc. A free catalog of The Ohio Experience Products is available by calling 800-536-2GET, or by visiting our website at: www.ohioexperience.com

ISBN
0-635-02504-3 (Paperback)
0-635-02505-1 (Hardcover)

Printed and bound in the United States of America.

OTHER OHIO EXPERIENCE™ TITLES:

- Ohio Experience Poster/Map
- Ohio Facts & Factivities! CD-ROM
- Let's Discover Ohio! CD-ROM
- The BIG Ohio Reproducible Activity Book
- My First Book About Ohio!
- Ohio Jeopardy!: Answers and Questions About Our State
- My First Pocket Guide: Ohio
- The Ohio Coloring Book
- Ohio "Jography!": A Fun Run Through Our State
- Ohio Stickers
- Ohio Biography Bingo Game
- Ohio Geography Bingo Game
- Ohio History Bingo Game
- Ohio State Stuff Bookmarks
- Ohio Millionaire GameBook
- Ohio Wheel of Fortune GameBook
- Ohio Survivor GameBook
- Ohio BIG State Wall Timeline
- Ohio State Student Reference Timeline

Contents

Introduction	vi
Ohio Firsts!	1
I Am the Great State of Ohio!	2–3
Famous Buckeyes	4–5
Cincinnati Chili	6–7
The Great Serpent Mound	8
Lake Erie	9
Women of Ohio	10
All-American Soap Box Derby	11
Ohio Place Names	12
Ohio Presidents	13–15
Ohio State Emblems	16–17
Ghost Stories	18–19
First Foods from Ohio	20
Newark's Little Drummer Boy	21
Ohio Inventions	22
Ohio Buckeye	23
Rock and Roll Hall of Fame	24
Captains of Industry	25
Canals	26
Swiss Cheese	27
Pro Football Hall of Fame	28–29
The Dog Pound	30
Ohio Archaeology	31
The Ohio River	32
United States Air Force Museum	33
The Underground Railroad	34
Victoria Woodhull	35
Lake Erie Shipwrecks	36
The Battle of Lake Erie	37
Marblehead Lighthouse	38–39
Orville and Wilbur Wright	40–41
Martha, the Last Passenger Pigeon	42
Cedar Point	43
Supplies and Provisions	44–45
Baseball's Opening Day	46
Johnny Appleseed	47
Ohio Festivals	48–49
Ohio's Amish Culture	50–51
Covered Bridges	52
World's Largest in Ohio	53
Ohio Trivia	54–55
About the Authors	56

introduction

Dear Reader,

OHIO is my favorite state! It is a state full of surprises around every bend in the road or the river! OHIO is such as unusual state. It was once at the crossroads of America's early history, as well as its pioneering heyday! OHIO is also a geographical wonder! The rivers, the Great Lakes, extraordinary farmland, inspiring cities, and a corner that would make you believe you were in New England!

OHIO is so fascinating because its people are so varied. You can meet an astronaut, an inventor, a soap box derby racer, a ballerina, an artist, an Amish farmer, a president, a carousel operator, a hot dog vendor, a rock star, a famous Native American, a baseball player, an Olympian, a ground-breaking scientist, and many, many others as you travel through OHIO'S fascinating past and present.

And what of OHIO'S future? Oh, that's up to you! That's why it's so important to learn about your state. To understand how it came to be, what it's up to now, and where it's headed. After all, you are part of that future—wherever you go and whatever you do in your lifetime.

You know, you have some really big shoes to fill! Whether that's ballet slippers, baseball cleats, workboots, fat, white astronaut footwear, or some other…learn all you can about OHIO and OHIOANS. You need OHIO and OHIO needs you. This book is designed to complement my Ohio Experience series which you may have discovered in your school or library? If so, you've learned lots of facts. So now, buckeye, let's learn even more about your wonderful state. I'll just bet you'll learn a thing or two you didn't know!

Happy reading,

Carole Marsh

Carole Marsh, for The OHIO Experience Team

The OHIO Experience

Ohio Firsts—Yea!

Ohio was the first to have a:

- Professional major league baseball team in the world—the Cincinnati Red Stockings in 1869
- National Football League team, the Canton Bulldogs
- Billionaire, John D. Rockefeller
- Kindergarten in the United States, Columbus
- State school for the blind in the United States, Columbus
- Dental school in the world, Bainbridge
- Woman admitted to college, Oberlin College
- African American admitted to college, Oberlin College
- Man orbit the earth, John Glenn
- Man walk on the moon, Neil Armstrong
- Woman to fly solo around the world, Jerrie Mock
- Woman to run for president, Victoria Woodhull
- Parachute jump, Dayton
- Electric traffic light in the United States, Cleveland, 1914
- Miss America, Mary Campbell
- Book of matches, Barberton
- Vacuum cleaner, Canton
- Broadcast by a president on radio, Warren G. Harding
- Ice cream cone rolling machine, Cleveland
- Public county library in the United States, Van Wert
- Boy Scouts of America, started by Daniel Beard
- 4-H club in the United States, started by A. B. Graham
- Successful blood transfusion, Dr. George Crile
- Public weather service, Cincinnati
- Gas powered auto, John Lambert in 1891
- Mechanical refrigerator, Dayton
- Automobile mail truck, Cleveland, 1899
- Shopping center in the United States, Columbus
- Airplane solo instrument landing, Dayton
- First full-time professional fire department in America, Cincinnati, 1853
- First city to be lit with electricity, Cleveland, 1879
- First African American to win an Olympic gold medal, DeHart Hubbard, 1924

The OHIO Experience

I Am the G

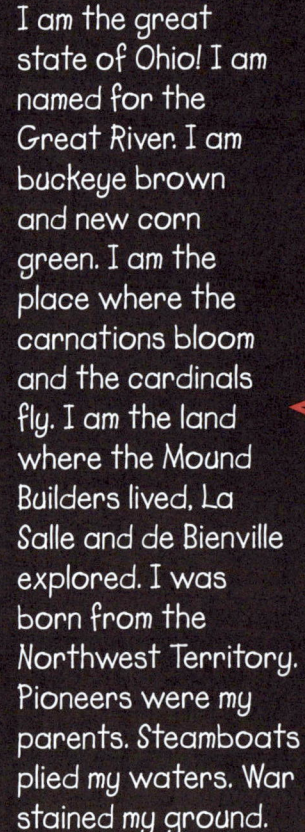

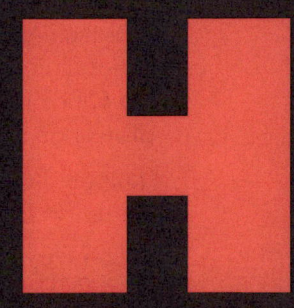

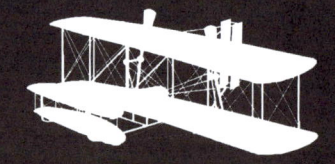

O I am the great state of Ohio! I am named for the Great River. I am buckeye brown and new corn green. I am the place where the carnations bloom and the cardinals fly. I am the land where the Mound Builders lived, La Salle and de Bienville explored. I was born from the Northwest Territory. Pioneers were my parents. Steamboats plied my waters. War stained my ground.

H I am the great state of Ohio. I hug a Great Lake. Canals connect my parts. I am known for socks that are red and skies that are blue. We look up! Up where the brothers Wright dreamed dreams that came true. Up where young astronauts took those dreams to the future.

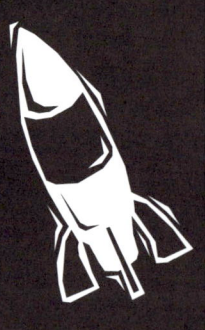

The OHIO Experience   3

Great State of OHIO!

I am the great state of Ohio. I am covered bridges and open plains. I am mansions on the river and bridges over the gaps. I am the bright land of invention. I am the Plain People and Rock and Roll! I am author and athlete. I am as slow as the trilobite and as fast as a racing boxcar!

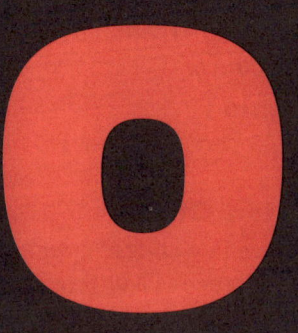

I am the great state of Ohio and I am fun! I am a rambling roller coaster and a cuckoo clock. I am as deep as a salt mine and as sparkling as a sulphur spring. I am places called Freedom and Delightful and Karamu. I am a mule-pulled barge and horse-drawn buggy. I am a senator in the statehouse and a student at a school desk. I am the place where all things are possible.

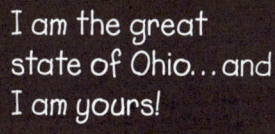

I am the great state of Ohio… and I am yours!

Activity: Try writing your own "I Am the Great State of Ohio!" Use strong verbs, vivid adjectives, color, sound, and smell!

by Carole Marsh

The OHIO Experience

FAM

Neil Armstrong (b. 1930) Wapakoneta, Ohio
This famous astronaut became the first person to walk on the Moon.

Halle Berry (b. 1968) Cleveland, Ohio
Halle Berry became the first African American woman to win the Best Actress Oscar.

Erma Bombeck (1927–1996) Dayton, Ohio
Erma Bombeck wrote humorous newspaper columns and books including At Wit's End and The Grass is Always Greener Over the Septic Tank.

Drew Carey (b. 1958) Cleveland, Ohio (Cuyahoga County)
Drew Carey is known for having his own television show and promoting the greater Cleveland area.

George A. Custer (1839–1876) New Rumley, Ohio
General George Armstrong Custer's unsuccessful attack on an Indian Village became known as "Custer's Last Stand."

Doris Day (b. 1924) Cincinnati, Ohio
This singer turned actress was born Doris Mary Ann Von Kappelhoff.

Thomas A. Edison (1847–1931) Milan, Ohio
Thomas Edison is given credit for inventing electric light, the motion picture camera, and many other useful inventions.

John Glenn (b. 1921) Cambridge, Ohio
In 1962, John Glenn became the first American to orbit the earth. Glenn served in the U.S. Senate from 1974–1999, and returned to space in 1998.

John Heisman (1869–1936) Cleveland, Ohio
The Heisman Trophy to recognize the nation's outstanding collegiate football player is named for this early football pioneer.

Toni Morrison (b. 1931) Lorain, Ohio
Toni Morrison is an African American author who has received many literary awards, among them the Pulitzer Prize in 1988.

BUCK

Annie Oakley (1860–1926) Patterson Township, Darke County, Ohio
Annie Oakley became a legendary sharpshooter while touring the country with Buffalo Bill and his Wild West Show.

Jesse Owens (1913–1980) Cleveland, Ohio
Jesse Owens, one of the greatest sprinters of all time, won four gold medals at the 1936 Olympics.

Pete Rose (b. 1941) Cincinnati, Ohio
The Major League Baseball record for highest number of career hits and highest number of games played are held by Pete Rose.

William Tecumseh Sherman (1820–1891) Lancaster, Ohio (Fairfield County)
Ranked second only to General Ulysses S. Grant as the greatest Northern general during the Civil War.

Steven Spielberg (b. 1947) Cincinnati, Ohio
Director of many films and winner of three Oscars for his direction of *Saving Private Ryan* and *Schindler's List*.

George Steinbrenner (b. 1930) Rocky River, Ohio
George Steinbrenner, one of the most successful owners in baseball, has led the New York Yankees to many World Series Championships.

Tecumseh (1768–1813) near present-day Columbus
Tecumseh was a Shawnee Indian Chief who fought against white settlement and tried to unite tribes to prevent further settlement.

Ted Turner (b. 1938) Cincinnati, Ohio
Known as a successful businessman and a cable-television pioneer, Ted Turner turned philanthropist in 1998 when he pledged $1 billion to the United Nations.

Cy Young (1867–1955) Gilmore, Ohio (Harrison County)
On May 5, 1905, in a baseball game against the Philadelphia Athletics, Cy Young pitched the first perfect game in American League history.

Cincinnati Chili

Cincinnati, Ohio, is one of the most chili-crazed cities in the United States. Cincinnati-style chili is a little different from what out-of-towners expect from chili. But folks in Cincinnati love it—there are about 180 chili parlors in the city alone. (Once they've tried it, many out-of-towners prefer Cincinnati chili to regular chili!)

The oldest Cincinnati chili parlor is the Empress. Tom and John Kiradjieff opened for business next door to the Empress Theater on Vine Street in 1922. Full of aromatic spices of his Greek homeland, Kiradjieff's recipe is traditionally served over hot spaghetti. No one knows for sure the exact blend of spices that he used; and today, the many chili parlors of Cincinnati all closely guard their recipes.

Most Cincinnati-chili connoisseurs agree on the basics of the recipe. The chili has a thinner consistency and is prepared with an unusual blend of spices that includes cinnamon, chocolate or cocoa, allspice, and Worcestershire.

2, 3, 4, or 5

Cincinnati chili lovers order their chili by number: Two-, Three-, Four-, or Five-Way. When making your own, let guests create their own final product.

Two-Way Chili: Chili served on spaghetti

Three-Way Chili: Additionally topped with shredded Cheddar cheese

Four-Way Chili: Additionally topped with chopped onions

Five-Way Chili: Additionally topped with kidney beans

Cincinnati Chili
(Makes 6 to 8 servings.)

1 large onion chopped
1 pound extra-lean ground beef
1 clove garlic, minced
1 tablespoon chili powder
1 teaspoon ground allspice
1 teaspoon ground cinnamon
1 teaspoon ground cumin
½ teaspoon red (cayenne) pepper
½ teaspoon salt
1 ½ tbsp unsweetened cocoa or ½ ounce grated unsweetened chocolate
1 (15-ounce) can tomato sauce
1 tablespoon Worcestershire sauce
1 tablespoon cider vinegar
½ cup water
1 (16-ounce) package uncooked dried spaghetti
Toppings (see opposite page)

- In a large frying pan over medium-high heat, sauté onion, ground beef, garlic, and chili powder until ground beef is slightly cooked. Add allspice, cinnamon, cumin, cayenne pepper, salt, unsweetened cocoa or chocolate, tomato sauce, Worcestershire sauce, cider vinegar, and water. Reduce heat to low and simmer, uncovered, 1 ½ hours. Remove from heat.

- Cook spaghetti according to package directions and transfer onto individual serving plates.

- Ladle chili over spaghetti and serve with toppings of your choice. Oyster crackers are served in a separate container on the side.

THE Great Serpent Mound

The Great Serpent Mound is located in rural Adams County, Ohio, east of Cincinnati. Stretching a quarter mile, Serpent Mound is the largest serpent effigy known to this day. The base of the mound is constructed of rock and clay. The soil that covers the rock is between four and five feet thick. The mound was built on top of a remarkably unique structure that has caused it to become misshapen over the years. Some people say the shape looks like a serpent with its mouth open about to eat an egg, while others say the serpent is about to eat a frog. The serpent extends to the west; because of this, some think that the oval represents the setting sun.

Researchers have found similarities between the previous Adena Indian habitats and the Great Serpent Mound. One indication that the Adena Indians built the mound is that the Adena burial grounds were located nearby. The Adena Indians are well known for their mounds. They lived in Ohio and parts of Kentucky and West Virginia. Serpent images carved on stone tablets have been found in the Adena Indian burial grounds. Excavations of Serpent Mound have found fragments of pottery, ashes, animal bones, and burnt stone. All of these things are evidence of occupation of the Adena Indians.

The function of Serpent Mound is somewhat mysterious. It is most likely a religious symbol. Symbolically, the serpent has stood for many things, such as eternity or evil. The Adena may have built the mound as a gift to their god or to ward off evil.

Fredric Ward Putnam was one of the first archaeologists to excavate the Great Serpent Mound. After he displayed his findings at the World's Fair in Chicago in 1893, the site became well known. Putnam was concerned that the Serpent Mound would be destroyed so he became part owner of the Historical Society of Ohio and helped to preserve the Serpent Mound so it can be viewed by anyone.

Today, the Great Serpent Mound is still a mystery—and is still open to the public!

Lake Erie

Lake Erie is named for the American Indian tribe that once lived along its southern shores. The French explorers, who first encountered the lake, called it *Lac du Chat* or Lake of the Cat for the wild panthers that once roamed the area.

Lake Erie ranks 4th among the 5 Great Lakes. The only Great Lake smaller is Lake Ontario. **Lake Erie** is the 11th largest lake in the world! Of the five Great Lakes, **Lake Erie** lies the farthest south, has the warmest water, and is the shallowest. The deepest point of **Lake Erie** is only 210-feet deep. Measured along its shoreline, **Lake Erie** runs for about three hundred miles. **Lake Erie** is the stormiest of all the Great Lakes because it is quickly stirred up by winds raging across it from Canada. These wind-blown tides (also called seiches) made life difficult for early Ohio farmers.

Making a Comeback!

By the end of the 1960s, **Lake Erie** was dying. The quality of the water was so bad that all swimming was forbidden. The natural plant and animal life of the lake was disappearing fast. The busy transportation throughout the lake was killing it. Wastes from factories, cities, and farms had been polluting the lake for over a hundred years. Poisons such as mercury were killing the lake's wildlife.

In the 1970s, Canada and the United States joined forces to clean up **Lake Erie**. Measures were taken to keep dangerous substances from entering the waters. Poisonous levels of mercury have decreased and species of fish that had almost disappeared returned. It seems that **Lake Erie** has been restored to life!

Here is a fun way to remember the names of the 5 Great Lakes—HOMES!

Huron   Ontario   Michigan   Erie   Superior

Women of Ohio

Florence Ellinwood Allen • Allen was the first elected female judge in the United States in 1920 and the first woman elected to the Ohio Supreme Court in 1922. President Roosevelt appointed her to a U.S. Court of Appeals in 1934, making her the first woman to hold the position. She was also the first woman to sentence a man to death—Frank Motto who was electrocuted in 1921.

Dr. Elizabeth Blackwell • Blackwell taught at a private school in Cincinnati. After her applications had been rejected twenty-nine times, she became the first woman in the United States to graduate from medical school in 1849. She graduated from Geneva Medical School in New York—first in her class!

Catherine Ewing • Ewing, a schoolteacher from Marietta, Ohio, founded the world's first public orphanage in 1867. "Aunt Katy Fay" paid the faculty out of her own pocket and worked for the Ohio legislation that established children's homes in every county.

Sally Jane Priesand • Ordained in 1972 at Cincinnati's Hebrew Union College—Jewish Institute of Religion, Sally Priesand became the first woman rabbi in the United States.

Susanna Madora Salter • At the age of 27, Salter became the first woman mayor in the United States. Voters in Argonia, Kansas elected this Belmont County native in 1887 by a two-thirds majority.

Lucy Sessions • Sessions was the first African American woman in the United States to earn a college degree—from Oberlin in 1850.

Victoria Claflin Woodhull • Woodhull was the first woman U.S. presidential candidate in 1872. She was also a newspaper publisher, a New York stockbroker, the first woman to speak before a congressional committee, and an advocate of women's rights.

The OHIO Experience   11

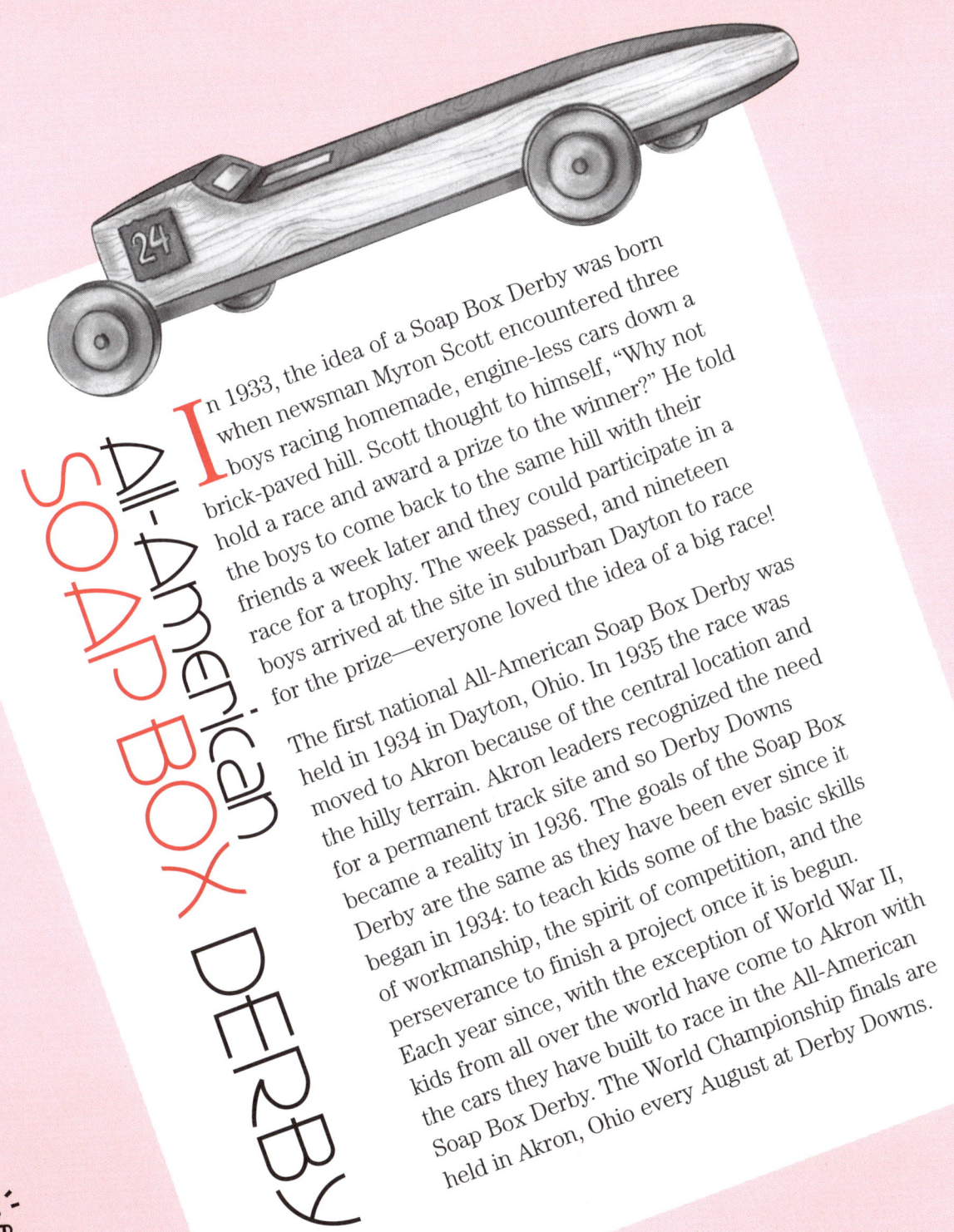

All-American SOAP BOX DERBY

In 1933, the idea of a Soap Box Derby was born when newsman Myron Scott encountered three boys racing homemade, engine-less cars down a brick-paved hill. Scott thought to himself, "Why not hold a race and award a prize to the winner?" He told the boys to come back to the same hill with their friends a week later and they could participate in a race for a trophy. The week passed, and nineteen boys arrived at the site in suburban Dayton to race for the prize—everyone loved the idea of a big race!

The first national All-American Soap Box Derby was held in 1934 in Dayton, Ohio. In 1935 the race was moved to Akron because of the central location and the hilly terrain. Akron leaders recognized the need for a permanent track site and so Derby Downs became a reality in 1936. The goals of the Soap Box Derby are the same as they have been ever since it began in 1934: to teach kids some of the basic skills of workmanship, the spirit of competition, and the perseverance to finish a project once it is begun. Each year since, with the exception of World War II, kids from all over the world have come to Akron with the cars they have built to race in the All-American Soap Box Derby. The World Championship finals are held in Akron, Ohio every August at Derby Downs.

A Gazetteer of Unique **Ohio Place Names**

Have you heard of these wonderful Ohio county, township, city, and village names? Perhaps you can start your own collection! (Place names appear in bold letters.)

Taking a **Bath** in **Coldwater** gives me the chills. It took going to **Remindersville** to remember that I was supposed to be doing summer **Reading**. Today's world news showed **Blue Ash** falling in **Poland**, causing quite a disturbance. After going round and round **Circleville**, I finally hung my head in **Defiance** because I just knew I was never going to make it home. My mother traveled to **Rootstown** to try to prove she was related to Marilyn **Monroe**. My sister was too afraid to walk among the **Seven Hills** in **Shaker Heights** because she was too scared she would fall. I found my husband, Old **McDonald** in **Loveland**. I grew up in **Coolville** but I had to move to **Newcomerstown** a few weeks ago; the people there are very nice. In my travels to **London** and **Athens**, I ran across many statues with **Marblehead**s. My **Mentor** was the man who taught me to claim my **Independence**. **Bowling Green** bean cans is not as easy as it may seem.

OHIO PRESIDENTS

While the first of these presidents were born on the Buckeye frontier, and the later ones were born in Ohio towns, they all have one thing in common. Ohio claims them as its own. Also of interesting note is that in the period between Reconstruction and the Roaring Twenties, there were ten presidents—seven of them were from Ohio. Perhaps this half-century period could be considered the time when Ohio ruled the nation. Here are the eight, great, late, Ohio presidents!

William Henry Harrison was the 9th president. When he was elected, he lived in North Bend, Ohio. His father, Benjamin Harrison V, signed the Declaration of Independence. Harrison was the first president to be photographed in office. President Harrison was a great speaker—so great, in fact, that his inaugural address lasted nearly four hours. Unfortunately, President Harrison made that speech in a freezing rain. He was the first president to die in office (of pneumonia)—after serving only one month in office, from March 4 to April 4, 1841. Ironically, he was also the first and only president who studied medicine.

Ulysses Simpson Grant was the 18th President. The General who commanded the Union Army to victory in the Civil War was born in Point Pleasant, Ohio in 1822. Grant was the first president to run against a woman (Victoria Woodhull). He served two full terms as president, from March 4, 1869 to March 3, 1877. During his administration, the 15th Amendment to the Constitution (which gave all qualified male citizens the right to vote) was ratified. He died on July 23, 1885.

More...

14 The OHIO Experience

Rutherford Birchard Hayes was the 19th President. Born in Delaware, Ohio, in 1822, Hayes was a major figure in Ohio politics. He was a Congressman from Ohio in the U.S. House of Representatives from 1865 to 1867. He was the Governor of Ohio for two terms: 1868–1872 and 1876–1877. President Hayes was the first to have a telephone installed in the White House in 1878. Hayes was the first president to visit the West Coast while in office, arriving September 8, 1880, in San Francisco. He served one term as president of the United States, from March 4, 1877 to March 3, 1881. He died in 1893.

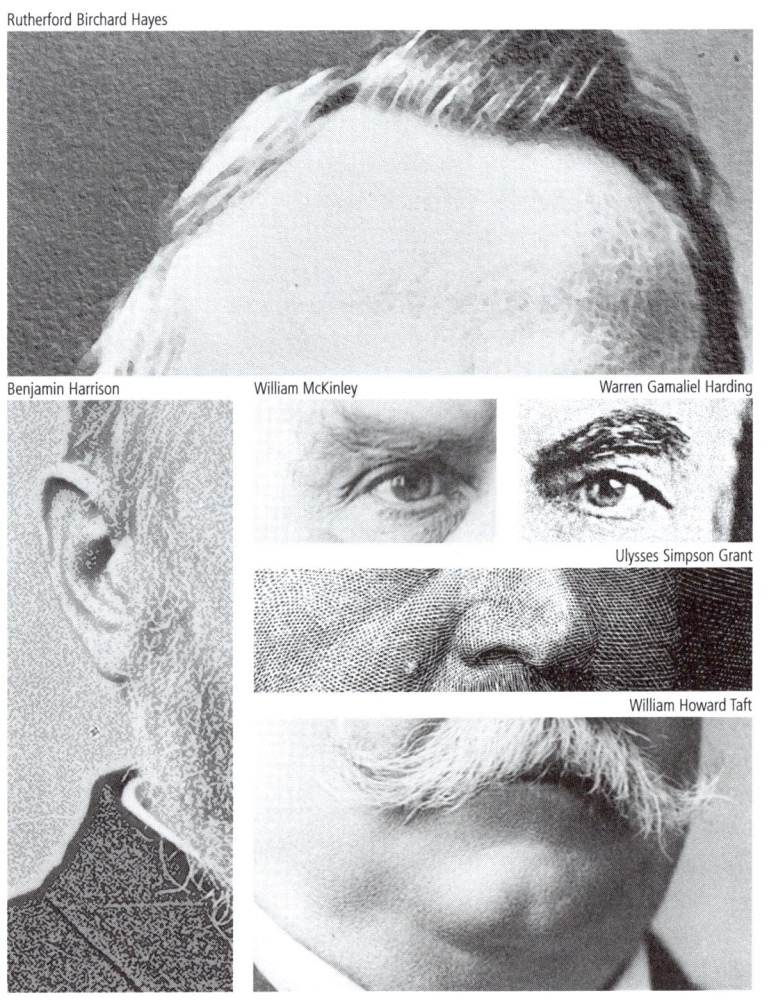

James Abram Garfield was the 20th President. Born in Cuyahoga County, Ohio, in 1831, Garfield was the last president born in a log cabin. He served in the Ohio State Legislative Service from 1859 to 1861, then was a Congressman from Ohio in the U.S. House of Representatives from 1863 to 1880. He then served only six months as President of the United States, from March 4 1881 to September 19, 1881; he was shot on July 2, and died on September 19. Garfield was the first president to have his mother at his inauguration. President Garfield was the first left-handed and ambidextrous president.

Rutherford Birchard Hayes

Benjamin Harrison

William McKinley

Warren Gamaliel Harding

Ulysses Simpson Grant

William Howard Taft

Do you recognize this famous U.S. president?

Benjamin Harrison was the 23rd President. The grandson of President #9 was born in North Bend, Ohio, in 1833. He served one term as president, from March 4, 1889 to March 3, 1893.

During his administration, six states joined the Union: North and South Dakota, Montana, Idaho, Wyoming, and Washington. Electric lights were installed in the White House during his presidency—but his First Lady never used them!

Harrison was the first president with a billion dollar budget. President Harrison was the first to put up a Christmas tree in the White House in 1889. He died on March 13, 1901.

William McKinley was the 25th President. He was born in Niles, Ohio in 1843. He was a Congressman from Ohio in the U.S. House of Representatives from 1877 to 1883, and from 1885 to 1891. He was Governor of Ohio from 1892 to 1896. McKinley was the first president to campaign over the telephone. He served one full term as president from 1897 to 1901. He was reelected to a second term which began on March 4, 1901, but was assassinated and died on September 14, 1901.

William Howard Taft was the 27th President. Born in Cincinnati, Ohio, in 1857, Taft served as president for one term, from March 4, 1909 to March 3, 1913. During his administration, New Mexico and Arizona became states, and the 16th Amendment to the Constitution was ratified. Taft, a lawyer, was the first president to serve on the U.S. Supreme Court after his presidency. He died on March 8, 1930, and was the first president to be buried at Arlington National Cemetery.

Warren Gamaliel Harding was the 29th President. Born in Blooming Grove, Ohio, in 1865, Harding served in the Ohio Senate, then as Lt. Governor of Ohio. He was a U.S. Senator from Ohio from 1915 to 1921. President Harding was the first president to be elected with the help of women voters. Harding was the first president to ride to his inauguration in an automobile, and the first president to visit both Alaska and Canada. He was also the first president to own a radio which he placed in his study. Harding served as president from March 4, 1921 to August 2, 1923, when he died of a heart attack.

16   The OHIO Experience

OHIO State EMBLEMS

State Animal – White-tailed Deer
Governor Richard F. Celeste made the white-tailed deer the state animal in 1988 after a fourth-grade class made the request.

State Tree – Buckeye

State Seal

State Wildflower – Large White Trillium
White trillium was used by Indians and early settlers to make medicines, such as astringents, tonics, and expectorants.

State Gem Stone – Flint
Flint is found in several parts of the state but especially on Flint Ridge. Native Americans would use the hard rock for knives, spearpoints, and arrowheads.

State Bird – Cardinal
The cardinal can be seen in Ohio year round.

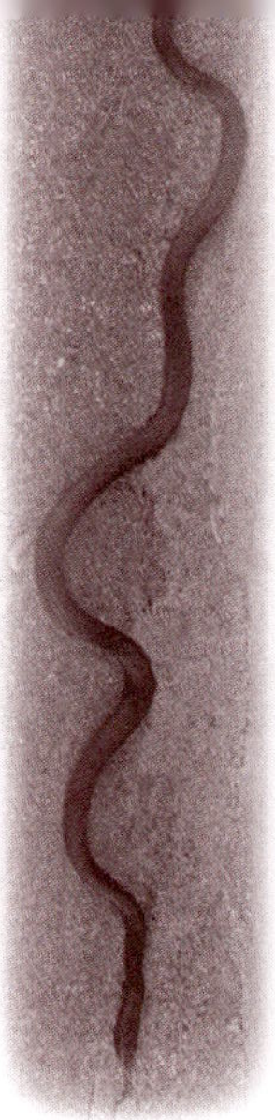

The OHIO Experience   17

**State Insect –
Ladybug**

State Flag
Ohio is the only state in the nation with a pennant-shaped flag.

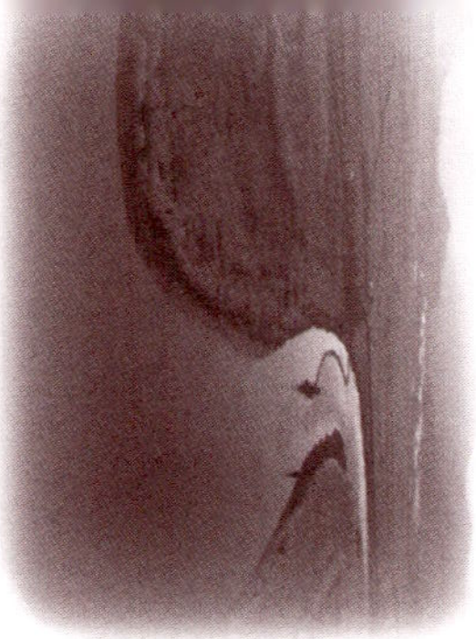

**State Song –
"Beautiful Ohio"**
Written in 1918 by Ballard McDonald and Mary Earl; the song is about the river, not the state.

**State Flower –
Scarlet Carnation**
President William McKinley, who was from Ohio, always wore a scarlet carnation in his buttonhole; adopted 3 years after he was assassinated in 1901.

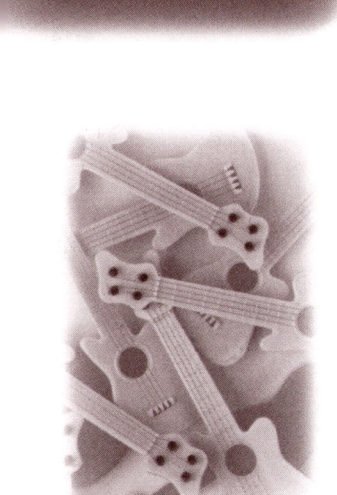

**State Rock Song –
"Hang on Sloopy"**

State Invertebrate Fossil – Trilobite

**State Reptile –
Black Racer Snake**

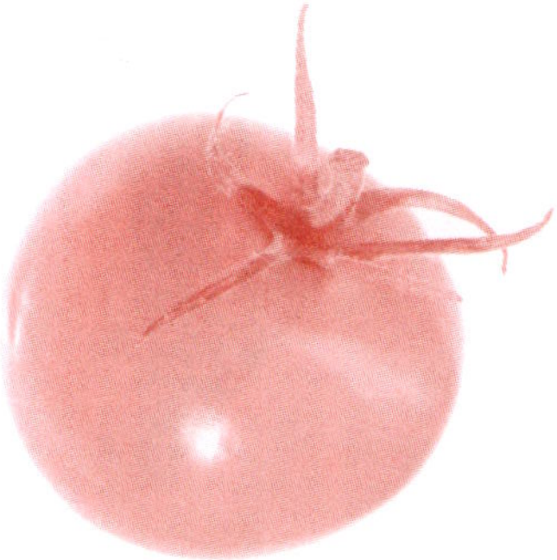

**State Beverage –
Tomato Juice**
A seed merchant, A.W. Livingston, from Reynoldsburg, Ohio developed the first edible tomato!

GHOST STORIES

Buxton Inn's Bonnie Ghost

According to legend, and the accounts of those who have had the pleasure of a meeting, the resident spirits at the Buxton Inn in Granville, Ohio are just continuing to play the roles of host and hostess. It is said that if the feminine fragrance of gardenias drifts heavily across the air on the stairway, the Lady in Blue is nearby. The spirit is better known as Ethel Bounell, or "Bonnie." The former actress turned innkeeper was the owner and operator of the inn for 26 years, from 1934 to 1960. The innkeeper died in room nine. According to the staff and guests, she is often heard walking up and down the stairs or opening and closing doors. Guests have reported being wakened by a woman concerned over their comfort.

While Bonnie is tending guests, she is not doing so alone. The first innkeeper, Major Buxton, also has appeared to both guests and staff. The gentleman is said to show up in the bar or to come up behind the staff, perhaps to make sure that all is running smoothly.

Sorg Opera House Ghost

More than a hundred years ago, Paul Sorg, a wealthy entrepreneur, built the Sorg Opera House in Middletown, Ohio. As owner, the well-dressed businessman is reported to have always claimed the best seat in the house, the first row of the first balcony, when he attended performances. Over the years and even today, staff and patrons claim to catch a glimpse of Sorg taking his seat in the first balcony. Sometimes his footsteps are heard walking along the stage or across the catwalks overhead.

The Lady in Gray

If you decide to take a stroll through the historic Camp Chase Confederate Cemetery in Columbus, some say the Lady in Gray might join you. A grieving young woman with her hair in a bun and dressed in a gray traveling suit is fabled to walk among the graves there. Visitors to the site have reported seeing the sad woman always looking down and weeping. Since the site is also home to Civil War re-enactments, the legend continues to grow. Those participating in the re-enactments and dressed in the period garb or uniform have reported either being joined by the Lady in Gray, hearing an otherworldly weeping, or having their commemorations interrupted by violent gusts of wind.

Bowling Green Ghost

Those attending a theater production at Bowling Green State University may, according to legend, meet the theater department's resident ghost—Alice. According to the superstitious, Alice must be invited to every performance. This must be a formal invitation by the stage manager, who must be alone on stage. If Alice is not consulted or thanked after the performance, actors report that she shows her temper by knocking over set pieces. Just who Alice is—or was—is also a legend. According to one of the most popular stories, Alice was a Bowling Green student and actress who, while on her way to receive an honor known as "Actress of the Year," was killed in a car crash before collecting her award. Another tale is that she was actually killed in the theater when a falling object cut short her performance in Othello. Those who have communicated with Alice say that she appears as a shadowy figure with long, flowing hair. It has also been said that she has returned in full costume when Othello is being performed, perhaps to finish the performance that she began so many years ago.

First Foods from Ohio

The Hamburger Frank Menches claimed to have invented the hamburger in the 1890s at the Summit County Fair. He had run out of sausages and told an assistant to "grind some beef"; therefore, giving us the modern day hamburger. **Life Savers** Cleveland chocolate maker Clarence Crane invented Life Savers in 1912. He gave the candies peppermint flavoring and sold them for a nickel, "for that Stormy Breath." **Rippled Potato Chips** Emerson Cain of Bowling Green claims to have invented the first rippled potato chips in the 1930s. **Girl Scout Cookies** In 1930, Girl Scouts in Akron were the first in the United States to engage a commercial bakery for their cookies. Albrecht Grocery Company made nearly a hundred thousand sandwich cremes stamped with a picture of Peter Rabbit. Within four years, all of the nation's Girl Scout cookies were bakery-made. **Chewing Gum** On December 28, 1869, the first patent issued for chewing gum was given to William Semple, a dentist from Mount Vernon, Ohio. His plan was to make gum out of rubber and other materials like chalk or charcoal to scour the teeth. Thank goodness Semple never manufactured his chewing gum—Yuck! **The Hot Dog** Harry M. Stevens of Niles, Ohio is credited with being the first person to put together a wiener with bread; this was called a "hot dog" after a New York newspaper caricatured the frankfurter as a dog in 1900. **Tomato** In 1870, Alexander Livingston of Reynoldsburg introduced the first palatable tomato. Before that, tomatoes were very tough and sour—some people even thought they were poisonous!

The OHIO Experience

Newark's little Drummer Boy

Approximately 320,000 Ohio men volunteered for service in the Civil War. Some of these men included General George H. Thomas, Colonel Lorin Andrews, and the infamous William Tecumseh Sherman. Several generals were important to Union successes, such as George B. McClellan, and Ulysses S. Grant. One of the most memorable volunteers proved to be just a boy. His name was Johnny Clem, and he was from a large family of German immigrants who had settled in Newark, Ohio. Johnny was only nine years old when the South bombarded Fort Sumter in 1861, but he told his parents he wanted to be a **drummer** boy for the soldiers departing the state. His parents reminded him that he was just nine, and his father said that he would need him to sell vegetables door-to-door later that summer. Johnny's mother sent him off to Sunday school, and he did not return. Instead, he hitched a train to Columbus and attempted to enlist as a **drummer**. Too young to be a **drummer**, he told the soldiers he was an orphan, and they made him their mascot. Johnny finally got a **drum** and helped the men keep good spirits on their way to the front. He witnessed action throughout the Tennessee River Valley and in a large battle, his **drum** was damaged by shellfire at Shiloh. From that day on he was known as Johnny Shiloh. Johnny Clem survived the war, received a service medal, and returned to Newark to finish grammar school.

Ohio Inventions

Stepladder
John Balsley,
Dayton, 1870

Incandescent Electric Light Bulb
Thomas Edison,
Milan, 1879

Airplane
Wilbur and Orville Wright,
Dayton, 1903

Cash Register
James S. Ritty,
Dayton, 1879

Play-Doh
Tien Liu and Joseph McVicker,
Cincinnati, 1950s

Artificial Fish Bait
Ernest Pflueger,
Akron, 1883

Automobile Self-Starter
Charles F. Kettering,
Dayton, 1911

Pop-Top Can
Ermal Fraze,
Dayton, 1965

Disposable Diapers (Pampers)
Procter & Gamble,
Cincinnati, 1962

Teflon
Roy Plunkett,
New Carlisle, 1938

Refrigerator with Door Shelves
"The Shelvador",
Powel Crosley, Jr.,
Cincinnati, 1933

Bicycle
Fisher A. Spofford and Matthew G. Raffington,
Columbus, 1869

Vacuum Cleaner
Murray Spangler,
Canton, 1907

Self-Lowering Toilet Seat
Gregory Janek,
Conover, 1986

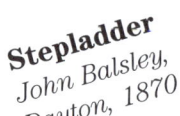

Floating Soap (Ivory)
Procter & Gamble,
Cincinnati, 1879

22 The OHIO Experience

Ohio Buckeye

The Ohio **Buckeye** tree is a tall tree growing up to 70 feet tall. It is generally found growing along rich, moist Ohio bottomlands, producing beautiful yellow flower spikes in April or May, later bearing a chestnut-like fruit. Though the flower spikes are beautiful, they give off an unpleasant odor. Native Americans called the fruit *hetuck*, meaning "the eye of the buck," for its dark center. The **buckeye** nut is not edible for humans, but squirrels are able to eat the fruit with no side effects. Carrying a **buckeye** nut is said to be good luck. Pioneers used **buckeye** wood to build cabins and furniture; its wood has also been used for making artificial limbs because of its lightness and workability.

The **buckeye** leaf blades are arranged like fingers on the palm of a hand.

Ohio Buckeye Candy

3 c. of creamy peanut butter
1 ½ sticks of softened butter
2 lbs. confectioners sugar
16-oz. chocolate chips, melted

Mix together peanut butter, butter, and confectioners sugar. Form into small balls. Using a toothpick, dip balls into melted chocolate until almost covered, leaving some of the peanut butter mixture exposed on top. Refrigerate and enjoy!

Rock and Roll Hall of Fame Museum

If you're ever in Cleveland and you happen to drive by a large geometric-shaped structure—STOP, in the name of rock and roll! It's the **Rock and Roll Hall of Fame and Museum!** Items owned by some of rock and roll's most famous performers are constantly on display. You can see a guitar once played by Buddy Holly, or look at some of the costumes once worn by the Supremes. Visitors can listen to all of their favorite rock and roll "oldies," and watch continuously-playing movies of early concert footage.

The **Rock and Roll Hall of Fame Foundation** was established in 1984 "to recognize these artists and their achievements in a dignified, uncommercial way." Many cities were considered for the site of the museum including Memphis, Philadelphia, Chicago, and New Orleans. Many of these cities have strong ties to the early history of rock and roll, so it was difficult to decide where the museum was to be located, but in the end, Cleveland was chosen.

Why Cleveland?

Alan Freed was one of rock and roll's first heroes. In 1951, he was a disc jockey at a Cleveland radio station. Using the nickname "Moondog," Freed began hosting a program of rhythm and blues music on station WJW. He began to call the music "rock and roll" after a popular song lyric. In March 1952, Freed held his "Moondog Coronation Ball" at the 10,000-capacity Cleveland Arena. More than 20,000 fans crashed the gates, causing the dance to be cancelled. This is considered by many to be the first "rock" concert.

Freed's radio show made him a national celebrity. He began starring in movies including *Rock Around the Clock* (1956), *Rock Rock Rock* (1956), *Don't Knock the Rock* (1956), and *Mr. Rock And Roll* (1957). Freed went on to host radio shows in New York and Los Angeles, but his career was marked with difficulties that many people believe led to an early death in 1965.

Before Elvis, Alan Freed was once called the "King of Rock and Roll," and is the reason Cleveland was chosen as the site for the **Rock and Roll Hall of Fame and Museum.**

The Rock and Roll Hall of Fame and Museum was designed by the famous architect, I.M. Pei.

Captains of Industry

Powell Crosley (1886–1961), born in Cincinnati, pioneered radio starting with low-powered transmitters and built it into Radio Station WLW, which broadcasted with 500,000 watts in the 1930s. He produced home appliances including a refrigerator with shelves on the door, called the "Crosley Shelvador." Crosley also manufactured a compact automobile called the "Crosley." In 1936, he purchased majority interest in the Cincinnati Reds baseball team and held that ownership until his death.

Thomas Alva Edison (1847–1931), born in Milan, is considered one of the world's greatest inventors. He took out 1,093 patents in his lifetime for such inventions as the incandescent electric lamp and the phonograph.

Harvey Samuel Firestone (1868–1938), born in Columbiana, was the founder and president of Firestone Tire & Rubber Company in Akron.

Benjamin Franklin Goodrich (1841–1888), pioneer rubber-goods manufacturer, opened a rubber-goods factory in Akron in 1870 that eventually became the B.F. Goodrich Company, maker of automobile tires.

Ransom Eli Olds (1864–1950), born in Geneva, was a pioneering manufacturer of automobiles. He built his first gas-operated car in 1896 and founded the Olds Motor Works in Detroit, Michigan (1899) to produce his "Oldsmobiles."

John D. Rockefeller, Sr. (1839–1937), Cleveland's first billionaire, was born in Richford, New York, but moved with his family to a farm near Cleveland. He is most famous for dominating the American oil-refining industry with his Standard Oil Company. Later in life, Rockefeller contributed to many charities and higher education institutions.

CANALS

When America was still young, the earliest explorers used rivers as water "highways." It was much faster to travel along waterways than to try to find one's way through the dense forests of the New World. New settlements bursting with pioneers sprang up near important lakes and rivers. However, some of these waterways were not connected. In order to move people and goods quickly from one place to another, canals were constructed between important cities.

From 1825 to 1847 more than 1,000 miles of canals were constructed in Ohio. The young state with its isolated frontier economy was transformed almost overnight. The canals opened markets for Ohio products and attracted thousands of immigrants to the state. Today only a few of the deep excavations and tall earthen embankments are left to remind us of Ohio's first important transportation system.

Traveling on a canal boat was not fast by modern standards. There was little or no current to help push the boat along. Instead the boat (also called a packet) was tied with a very long rope to a team of mules or horses. The animals walked along roads that lined the canal while pulling the boats along the canal. A canal driver was responsible for walking along with the team of animals and helping keep them going. The hardest job of all was to make sure the animals did not fall in the canal—and to help them out if they did!

From "Ohio Canal Song"

*Tramp, tramp, tramp, tramp;
 tighten up your line,
Watch the playful horseflies as on
 the mules they climb.
Whoa back, cuss the mules, forget it
 I never shall,
For I'm every inch a sailor on the
 Ohio Canal!*

From "Low Bridge, Everybody Down (The Erie Canal)"

*Low bridge, everybody down!
Low bridge, for we're comin'
 through a town!
And you'll always know
 your neighbor,
You'll always know your pal,
If you've ever navigated on the
 Erie Canal.*

Swiss Cheese

Americans call it **Swiss** cheese, but the **Swiss** call it *Emmenthaler*. The English and French call it *Gruyère*. Most Ohioans have another word to describe it—delicious! **Swiss** cheese is one of the nation's favorite cheeses, and Ohio is one of the top producers of **Swiss** cheese. At one time, there were nearly 300 cheese factories in Ohio. Although many factories have converted to more modern facilities, they still produce about 53,000,000 pounds of cheese per year. Ohio cheesemakers have combined their natural talent with years of experience to produce the finest **Swiss** cheese anywhere.

Early **Swiss** immigrants brought the cheese-making trade to Ohio. They learned the art in their homeland and brought it to Ohio beginning in about the 1830s. You can easily recognize **Swiss** cheese by the holes. Cheese makers refer to these holes as "eyes." **Swiss** cheese is still made in large wheels. Each wheel is floated in a brine tank for several days to produce a rind. The wheels can weigh between 160–200 pounds. Because of this, **Swiss** Cheese has earned the nickname, "King of Cheese." Today, Ohio cheesemakers also make blocks of **Swiss** cheese that are encased in plastic and weigh in at about 90 pounds.

Ohio Swiss Festival

Each October in the small town of Sugarcreek, Ohio, the annual Ohio **Swiss** Festival occurs. Switzerland itself could not be more **Swiss** than Sugarcreek with its symphony of **Swiss** music, authentic **Swiss** costumes, and authentic alpine business district. Tons of **Swiss** cheese from 7 local cheese-making plants and numerous other gourmet items may be purchased while visitors watch parades and continuous entertainment. Don't forget to see the unique **Swiss** athletic events such as the *Steinstossen* (stone throwing) and *Schwingfest* (**Swiss** wrestling). Visitors can also dance to top polka bands.

PRO FOOTBALL HALL OF FAME

The Pro Football Hall of Fame in Canton, Ohio honors the best players the game has produced. The Pro Football Hall of Fame is actually the National Football League's Hall of Fame. The Hall of Fame opened in 1963 with 17 charter inductees. Football champions are honored with bronze busts of themselves placed in the Hall of Fame. Nearby life-sized sketches show them punting, passing, running, or tackling and each year since 1963 new members have been elected to the Football Hall of Fame. In order to be considered for Hall of Fame status, a player must be retired for at least five years.

But the Hall of Fame is more than just an annual dinner and an inductee ceremony. The original building finished in 1963 has been joined with the addition of several other buildings. New displays and the long-awaited Game Day Stadium showing the "100-Yard Universe," an NFL Films production, were the final pieces in the expansion puzzle.

There are several reasons why Canton, Ohio was chosen for the Pro Football Hall of Fame. First, the American Professional Football Association, the direct forerunner of the National Football League, was founded in Canton in 1920. But even before that, the Canton Bulldogs were an early-day pro-football powerhouse, claiming several unofficial championship titles. They were also a two-time champion of the NFL in 1922 and 1923. Lastly, early in the 1960s Canton citizens launched a determined and well-organized campaign to earn the Pro Football Hall of Fame site designation for their city.

A 20TH CENTURY LEGEND

Jim Thorpe, the first big-name athlete to play pro football, played his first game with the Canton Bulldogs, beginning in 1915. An American Indian, Thorpe was one of the greatest all-around athletes in history. In the 1912 Olympic Games, he was the first athlete to win both the pentathlon and the decathlon. From 1913 to 1919, Thorpe played as an outfielder on three major league teams. In 1920, Thorpe became the first president of the American Professional Football Association, now known as the National Football League. Today, a graceful seven-foot bronze statue of Jim Thorpe greets visitors as they go into the Hall.

The Dog Pound

Cleveland Browns fans get excited whenever the end of summer draws near and it's time for football season to pick up again. As a group, fans are called the dog pound; their fist-pumping battle cry is the instantly recognizable, "Woof, Woof, Woof." (Out-of-towners might recognize this cheer as one borrowed by Cleveland native Arsenio Hall for his late night talk show.)

What makes the Browns different from any other team in the National Football League is their history. In 1995, Browns owner Art Modell announced he was relocating the team to Baltimore, Maryland. Browns fans were crushed; most fans felt that the team belonged to them and the city of Cleveland.

Just when it seemed as if the NFL and the Browns were going to leave the city forever, Cleveland and the NFL secured a deal for the Cleveland Browns to return to the playing field in 1999. Art Modell was taking his franchise with him, but there would be a new team in Baltimore. The deal stated that the name, colors, and heritage of the Browns would remain in Cleveland. This was the first time that any deal like this had happened in the NFL.

Many of those in the "dog pound" were not happy to see the old Cleveland Municipal Stadium go. The original "dog pound" was the bleachers directly behind the end zone in the old stadium. But the city had plans for a new stadium, Cleveland Browns Stadium, on the site where Cleveland Municipal Stadium was located. On September 12, 1999, the "new" Browns made their NFL debut. The fans have returned as well, bringing with them some of the old traditions from the past. Sometimes fans have been known to throw dog bones onto the field during the game and dress up like bulldogs!

How did the Cleveland Browns get their name?

The Cleveland Browns were named for the extremely popular coach, Paul Brown. At first, Coach Brown did not think it was proper for the team to be named after him. Eventually he agreed, but modestly stated in public that the team was named for boxer, Joe Louis, who was nicknamed "The Brown Bomber."

Cleveland Browns Stadium

mammal fossils

ground sloths

These mammals were slow moving plant eaters. They were similar to the South American tree sloths of today, but they lived on the ground. This mammal fossil has only been found in two places in Ohio. In 1890, a skeleton of a ground sloth was found in Holmes County. The skeleton is 11-feet long and 7-feet tall. The skeleton is on display in the Orton Geological Museum on the Ohio State University campus.

stag moose

This mammal fossil was from the ice age and was similar to the modern-day moose. The difference is that the stag moose was more slender than a moose of today. The stag moose also had more complex antlers. These animals most likely fed on water plants in glacial lakes. There have only been five of these mammals found in Ohio, the first one being found in Darke County in the early 1970s. An almost complete skeleton was found in 1987 in Stark County and is displayed at the Ohio Historical Center in Columbus.

mastodons and mammoths

These big, elephant-like herbivores are the largest mammal fossils to be found in Ohio. Mastodons fed on twigs, branches, and other plants. Mammoths would feed on grasses and other vegetation. The bones of the two mammals look very much alike but can be distinguished by their teeth. A mastodon tooth has mound-like cusps and bulges. A mammoth tooth is made up of flat, plate-like portions. The Conway Mastodon was found in 1898 in Clark County and is displayed at the Ohio Historical Center in Columbus. Fossil remains of nearly 250 of these mammals have been found in Ohio.

THE OHIO RIVER

One look at a map of Ohio and anyone can easily identify the Ohio River—the river marks the southern boundary of the state. It was the Iroquois who first named the river, O-Y-O, or the "great" river. Other ancient Indians left evidence of their mound-building culture all through the Ohio River valley.

The first European to see the Ohio River may have been Frenchman René Robert Cavelier, Sieur de La Salle around 1669–1670 although some scholars disagree on whether it was the Ohio or another river he named *la belle riviere* or the "beautiful" river. At any rate, by the 1700s, the Ohio River was an important crossroads between American Indians, French traders, American settlers, and the British government. All of these groups fought to control this region because they knew the area was rich with natural resources and was an important transportation route.

During the 1800s, the Ohio River became a water highway for farmers in Ohio, Kentucky, Indiana, and Illinois. Canals and turnpikes linked many parts of Ohio to the river. Farmers could send their crops much more quickly and cheaply to the major cities along the East Coast by sending them down river to the Mississippi River and eventually on down to New Orleans. From there, goods were placed on ocean-going ships and sent around the tip of Florida and up the eastern seaboard to major cities. Although this may seem out of the way, it was actually shorter than loading their merchandise on horse-drawn wagons and sending them over the Appalachian Mountains.

Many of the first boats to travel the Ohio River were keelboats, made famous by the likes of Mike Fink and other "river rogues." It wasn't long before the first steamboat made its appearance on the Ohio River in 1811. The boat, *New Orleans*, set sail from Pittsburgh and steamed all the way down to New Orleans, Louisiana. Cincinnati soon emerged as an important center for steamboat building.

Railroads, trucks, or planes have replaced much of the river traffic, but they will never replace the Ohio River completely. New locks and canals have made it much easier to travel on the Ohio River. While many of the keelboats and steamboats of yesterday have been replaced with modern river-going vessels, the Ohio River remains one of the United States' most important transportation routes.

The Ohio River Museum in Marietta, Ohio preserves some of the rich history of the river.

United States AIR FORCE Museum

Dayton, Ohio is often called the "Birthplace of Aviation." During the 1890s, brothers Wilbur and Orville Wright operated a bicycle shop in Dayton while they tried to build the first successful flying machine. Wright-Patterson Air Force Base is not far from the field where the Wright brothers conducted their first experiments with flight. On the grounds of the base is the United States Air Force Museum, the world's largest and oldest military aviation museum.

More than 350 aircraft and missiles, along with thousands of artifacts are on display at the 17-acre United States Air Force Museum. These exhibits present the history of military aviation from the first pioneers and their daring adventures to aircraft development of today's jets and their changing progress in design and engineering.

On display with the aircraft are military uniforms dating back to 1916 and personal mementos, such as diaries and medals. The museum was established in 1923 at McCook Field near Dayton, and was relocated to Wright Field in 1927. Due to the urgent need for administrative space to support the war effort, the museum closed its doors to the public from 1940 to 1955.

Among the many exhibits the museum has to offer is the B-25 exhibit, which depicts the accounts of those who served during the World War II "Tokyo Raid" mission. Resting on a simulated carrier deck, the B-25B comes to life with mannequins representing Lieutenant Colonel Jimmy Doolittle, members of the Doolittle Raiders and *USS Hornet* crewmembers. The museum staff spent nearly 5,000 hours on this one exhibit to ensure that every last detail was perfect. Other items of interest include a display devoted to Major Glenn Miller's Army Air Force Band and an original Wright wind tunnel. A special section of the Museum pays tribute to celebrities in uniform, including Brigadier General Jimmy Stewart, Major Clark Gable, Flight Officer Jackie Coogan, Captain Ronald Reagan, and Technical Sergeant Joe Louis.

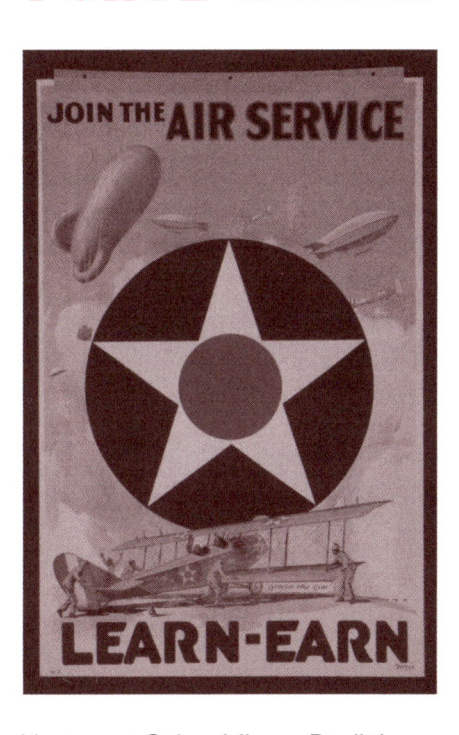

The museum staff continues to find new exciting ways to create exhibits by their research and sometimes from personal experiences.

The Underground Railroad

Because of its long river border with the state of Kentucky, Ohio played an important role in helping runaway slaves go north in pre-Civil War days. The network that helped fugitives flee toward Canada and safety was known as the Underground Railroad. The Underground Railroad wasn't a real railroad. Although it had no tracks or railroad cars, it did have "conductors." These were people who helped runaway slaves escape to freedom. By 1840, Ohio led all other states in Underground Railroad stations.

One Cincinnati resident was nicknamed "the president of the Underground Railroad." Levi Coffin belonged to a religious group called the Quakers that did not believe in slavery. Coffin grew up in North Carolina where he helped many slaves escape north. Eventually Coffin moved north and settled in Cincinnati, Ohio. It was a group of bitter Southern slaveholders who first gave him his nickname.

The Underground Railroad had numerous lines—possibly 500 routes in Ohio alone! One of the reasons that so many slaves came through Ohio was that parts of the Ohio River froze over in the winter and made it easier to cross into freedom. But, once a runaway slave made it into Ohio didn't mean that they were home free. There was still a chance they could be captured and returned to a slave state. Conductors on the Underground Railroad often helped the runaways escape to Canada or even as far away as Europe.

The National Underground Railroad Freedom Center is located on the banks of the Ohio River between the Great American Ballpark and Paul Brown Stadium in Cincinnati, Ohio. Displays in the "Pavilion of Perseverance" include the story of a female slave who escaped to Ohio by crossing the partly frozen Ohio River with her baby, inspiring Harriet Beecher Stowe—a preacher's daughter who lived in Cincinnati—to write "Uncle Tom's Cabin."

Victoria Woodhull
First Woman Presidential Candidate

Born in Homer, Ohio, Victoria Woodhull was considered very beautiful although many people considered her wild and eccentric. As a child she traveled throughout Ohio with her parents, giving spiritualist demonstrations. Her parents encouraged Victoria to see visions and hold seances.

When Victoria was still young, she married Dr. Canning Woodhull, but continued to tour. (Victoria later divorced Woodhull, but kept his name.) In 1868, the financier Cornelius Vanderbilt helped establish Woodhull's brokerage firm on Wall Street—first woman-owned brokerage! Newspapers nicknamed her "The Queen of Finance."

The news about Woodhull spread quickly around the country, and in 1870 she began publishing a reformist journal. It was her hope that her publication would help American women win more rights. Above all, the newspaper shared the idea that women could live as men's equals in the workplace, politics, church, and the family.

In 1871, Woodhull surprised the nation by presenting to Congress a statement claiming that women already had the right to vote! She was the first woman to make a presentation to the Congress. In 1872, Woodhull formed the Equal Rights party, which nominated her for the U.S. presidency. (She was beat by another Ohioan—Ulysses S. Grant!)

Eventually Woodhull decided to move to England where she married a wealthy Englishman, gave lectures occasionally, and continued to publish. Woodhull died in 1927 at her country estate near Tewkesbury, Gloucestershire, England.

Who was Victoria Woodhull's choice for Vice President?

Shortly after the passage of the Fifteenth Amendment giving all men the right to vote regardless of their color, Frederick Douglass seemed a natural choice for Woodhull's running mate. Douglass was a well-known abolitionist who had been born into slavery and spent most of his life fighting for the rights of American minorities.

"More Than Average Rough"

"More than average rough" is how one nineteenth-century ship captain described the conditions of Lake Erie. Of course the conditions can be quite calm and peaceful, but a rushing wind blowing south can change the conditions almost instantly. In the summer of 1826, Thomas McKenny, an agent of the Indian Department, set out on a trip up the Lakes to negotiate a treaty with the Chippewa at Fond du Lac on Lake Superior. Arriving in Detroit, he immediately began writing a description of Lake Erie. "Lake Erie…is a vast sea, and often more stormy, and even dangerous, than the ocean itself."

There are no fewer than 1,700 shipwrecks lying in Erie's shallow waters. But one particular storm marks the most terrible day for shipwrecks in Lake Erie's history. The date was October 20, 1916—it became known as Black Friday. There were four boats caught out on the lake that day: the schooner *D.L. Filer*, the lumber hooker *Marshall F. Butters*, the Canadian steamer *Merida*, and the whaleback freighter *James B. Colgate*. All four ships were sunk by the storm. Only three captains lived to tell the story; two of the three were the only survivors having helplessly watched their entire crews perish.

Perhaps the saddest of these four doomed ships is the story of Captain Mattison of the *D.L. Filer*. The ship had left Buffalo loaded with coal for a port on Lake Michigan. She nearly beat the storm, but was caught as she neared the Detroit River. The schooner was beaten by the waves until she broke apart and sank, 18 feet below the surface. After surviving a night of the storm by clinging to a mast poking out from the water, the captain and a crewmember were to be rescued. Just as they were about to be pulled aboard a passenger boat that happened to be passing by, the crewmember lost his grip and fell below the surface of the water, never to reappear. Captain Mattison, a skipper without a crew or a ship, was the lone survivor of the *D.L. Filer*.

Schooner tow song, c.1890

We leaves Detroit behind us,
We set our canvas tight;
The tug slows up and casts us off,
Old Erie heaves in sight!

So we watch our tiller closer,
We keep our sheet ropes clear;
There's no such thing as steady wind
Along Lake Erie here.

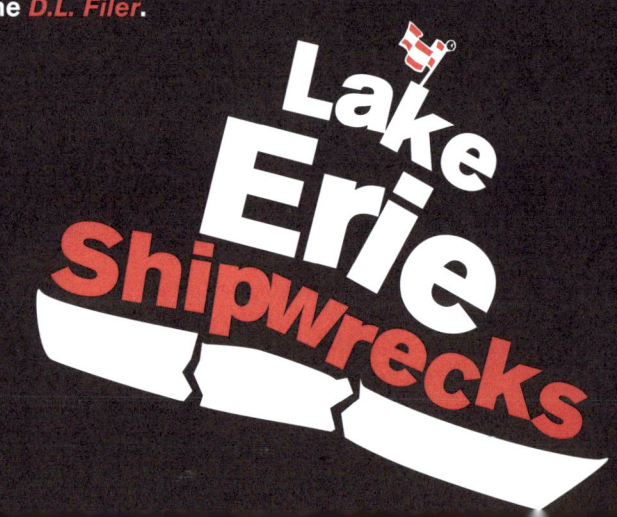

Lake Erie Shipwrecks

"We Have Met the Enemy and They Are Ours."

The Battle of Lake Erie

During the War of 1812, Commodore Oliver Hazard Perry was assigned to oversee the building of an American fleet at the eastern end of Lake Erie. He was only 28 years old at the time. In four short months, he had overseen the construction of nine ships equipped to carry 54 guns. Soon after, Robert H. Barclay, veteran British commander, sailed east from Malden, a port near Detroit, with six warships carrying 63 guns.

The two rivals met near Put-in-Bay, Ohio on September 10, 1813. The British took an early advantage, destroying Perry's flagship *Lawrence*. Perry then transferred to the *Niagara*, which had suffered little damage, and continued the fight. The battle lasted three hours. Perry lost 27 men, Barclay 41. An estimated 100 were wounded on both sides. The battle was a complete victory for the Americans. It was the first time in history that an entire British fleet was defeated and completely captured by an enemy.

After the British fleet surrendered, Perry reported his victory to General William Henry Harrison at Fort Meigs with the memorable words: "We have met the enemy and they are ours." That famous quotation refers to a battle that was more important than winning just a battle, and even more important than winning control of the Great Lakes. During the War of 1812, the United States was very close to losing the Northwest Territory. (At that time the Northwest referred to the area of present-day Ohio, Indiana, Illinois, Michigan, and Wisconsin.) Commodore Perry's fleet defeating the British was the main reason for the return of this territory to the United States at the peace conference at Ghent after the war. Perry brought back every British ship to his base as a prize of war. The public hailed Perry as a national hero for his victory on Lake Erie.

Even the Losers Get Lucky Sometimes!

Commander Robert H. Barclay the British commander at the Battle of Lake Erie was court-martialed. Barclay, who had years before sacrificed an arm while fighting the French, lost the use of his remaining arm in the Battle of Lake Erie. His pathetic appearance at the court-martial drew tears from spectators. Barclay was found not guilty of any blame for the loss of the British fleet on Lake Erie. He later became a full navy captain in the British fleet, got married, and had eight children!

Marblehead Lighthouse

Marblehead Lighthouse. Originally called the Sandusky Bay Lighthouse, Marblehead Lighthouse is the oldest lighthouse in continuous operation on the Great Lakes and has guided sailors along the Marblehead Peninsula since 1822. In 1819, the U.S. Congress recognized the need for a navigational aid along the Great Lakes and set aside $5,000 for the construction of a light tower at the entrance to Sandusky Bay. William Kelly built the 50-foot tower of limestone at the tip of Marblehead Peninsula. The base of the tower is 25 feet in diameter, with walls 5-feet thick. The lighthouse narrows at the top to 12 feet in diameter with walls 2-feet thick.

A Fresnel Lens

The Lightkeepers. In the history of the Marblehead Lighthouse, there have been fifteen lighthouse keepers—two of which were women. The first keeper was Benejah Wolcott, one of the first settlers on the peninsula. Each night he would light the wicks of thirteen whale oil lamps. Other duties included keeping a log of passing ships, noting weather conditions, and organizing rescue efforts. After Wolcott's death in 1832, his wife Rachel took over.

New Technology. In 1858 the light from a kerosene lantern that was magnified by a Fresnel lens replaced the oil lamps. This lens was a specialized, curved glass lens that created a highly visible, fixed white light. The turn of the century brought in new technology and new structural changes including the addition of 15 feet to the tower's height. A clock-like mechanism was installed to rotate the lantern, which created a bright flash of light every 10 seconds. This system required the lighthouse keeper to crank the weights every three hours through the night to keep the lantern turning.

Signs of the Times. In 1923 an electric light replaced the kerosene lantern which dramatically increased the power of the signal. During World War II the lighthouse became important for national defense. In 1946 the last civilian lighthouse keeper resigned and the U.S. Coast Guard assumed responsibility. In 1958, the beacon was automated and the lighthouse received a fresh coat of stucco. **Today.** The Ohio Department of Natural Resources has kept up the property surrounding the lighthouse and proudly accepted ownership in 1998. Today's modern lens projects a green signal that flashes every six seconds. The green light distinguishes the lighthouse from the white lights coming from air beacons.

OTHER OHIO LIGHTHOUSES

Name	Date Established	Height	Operational
Ashtabula	1836	40 ft	yes
Fairport Breakwater	1925	42 ft	yes
Fairport Harbor	1825	67 ft	no
Huron Harbor	1835	72 ft	yes
Lorain	1837	51 ft	no
Port Clinton	1900	20 ft	no
South Bass Island	1897	60 ft	no

Orville and Wilbur Wright Step Out into the Sky!

It is a cold winter's day. It is, in fact, December 17, 1903—a day that will go down in history. But brothers Orville and Wilbur Wright do not care about that at the moment.

Standing on the gigantic sand dune called Kill Devil Hill in Kitty Hawk, North Carolina, the two brothers shiver in the icy wind. They traipse across the blowing sand to the **Flyer**, their flying machine. At least they are counting on it to fly…this time.

It is Orville's turn to fly the plane. He cranks up the engine of the rather rickety-looking contraption that to some, perhaps, appears more an overgrown toy crafted of fabric and sticks. Like two gentlemen bidding one another farewell on a journey, the brothers shake hands.

Orville stretches out face-down on the bottom wing. Wilbur holds the tip of the wing steady. One of their helpers from the nearby Life Saving Station releases the wire that holds **Flyer** to the frozen ground.

Orville and Wilbur Wright, two brothers from Dayton, made the world's first flight in

The OHIO Experience   41

**At last,
at last
success!**

The craft is aloft... moving through the sky... heading into history.

Instantly, **Flyer** begins to roll forward on its launching rail. Faster, faster, ever faster, until—**EUREKA!**

wer-driven, heavier-than-air machine (an airplane), which they invented and built.

Martha, the Last Passenger Pigeon

A young boy named Press Southworth stood in his parents' barnyard near rural Sargents, in southern Ohio's Pike County. March 24, 1900 seemed a day like any other. The temperature was about 55 degrees and as many boys did, he begged his mother to let him shoot a strange bird that was eating corn on the family farm.

"I found the bird perched high in the tree and brought it down without much damage to its appearance," Southworth wrote 68 years later at the age of 82. "When I took it to the house Mother exclaimed, 'It's a passenger pigeon!'"

There were once billions of passenger pigeons in the United States. This seems hard to believe, but by all accounts true. Before the late 1800s, passenger pigeons were everywhere. Migrating flocks would block out the sun. Tree branches would break under their weight. Measured from tip-of-beak to tip-of-tail, the bird was about 15–17 inches long. Passenger pigeons could fly faster than a mile a minute. But they also tasted good, and the bird was mercilessly hunted.

The last passenger pigeon was named Martha. She was born (and died) at the Cincinnati Zoo. By the time that Martha was a teenager, she had become a popular tourist attraction. It was clear that she was the last passenger pigeon, and scientists frantically tried to breed her, offering thousands of dollars to anyone who would come forward with a mate. From 1909 to 1912, the American Ornithologists' Union offered $1,500 to anyone finding a nest or nesting colony of passenger pigeons. They also tried to breed her with other pigeon species, but had no luck.

At about one o'clock on September 1, 1914, Martha was found dead at the bottom of her cage. Her body was packed in ice and sent to The National Museum of Natural History in Washington, D.C., where she can still be seen on the first floor.

The Passenger Pigeon Memorial, a National Historic Landmark, is in a quiet corner of the Cincinnati Zoo. It displays a plaque of Martha, as well as the body of the last wild passenger pigeon ever documented—which was shot by Press Clay Southworth on March 24, 1900, near Sargents, Ohio.

The OHIO Experience 43

CEDAR POINT

Cedar Point is home to a world-record-breaking 16 roller coasters! The park had been called the "Best Amusement Park in the World" in an annual survey conducted by "Amusement Today." Cedar Point is the second oldest amusement park in North America, dating back to 1870. It is located in Sandusky, Ohio, in-between Cleveland and Toledo.

The Roller Coasters

1964 ~ Blue Streak
1969 ~ Cedar Creek Mine Ride
1970 ~ WildCat
1976 ~ Corkscrew
1978 ~ Gemini
1979 ~ Jr. Gemini
1987 ~ Iron Dragon
1989 ~ Magnum XL-200
1990 ~ Disaster Transport
1991 ~ Mean Streak
1994 ~ Raptor
1996 ~ Mantis
1999 ~ Woodstock Express
2000 ~ Millennium Force
2002 ~ Wicked Twister
2003 ~ Top Thrill Dragster

Fast Facts

- One lap around the park is 2.1 miles.
- The Cedar Point peninsula is 364 acres.
- The main parking lot is 64 acres.
- The oldest existing park building is the Convention Center, built in 1888 as the Grand Pavilion.
- Out of the approximately 4,500 seasonal employees, about 3,000 are housed at Cedar Point.
- There are over 2,000 trashcans along the main midway, Frontier Trail, Frontiertown, and in Challenge Park.

Supplies and Provisions: Ohio Stuff from the Past

In the Home · Apple peeler · Baskets and brooms · Butter churner · Canning jars, crocks, and bottles · Tea kettle · Sugar hatchet · Rolling pin · Boot jack · Ink stand · Coal scuttle · Wig block · Wash hand basins · Candle snuffer · Taper candlesticks · Copper boiler · Tea jug · Washing tub · Drying horse · Chests and trunks · Pewter plates · Quilts and blankets · Chamber pot · Cake soap · Clothes brush · Scissors

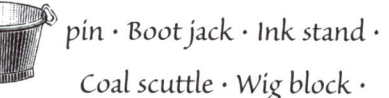

On the Farm · Axe · Hatchet · Hayrake · Weeding knife · Watering pot · Hoe · Scythe · Pitching fork · Wheelbarrow · Spade · Sledge and mattock · Plough · Harrow

To Wear · High-button shoes · Longjohns · Cotton, flannel, and linen "drawers" · Wigs · Leather breeches · Waistcoats · Cloaks and coats · Ruffled shirts · Silk cravat · Suit of mourning with weepers · Black worsted stockings · Wash leather, kid, and doe skin gloves · Cocked hats

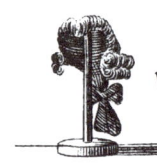

The OHIO Experience 45

Today in Ohio, we use the very latest in high-tech gadgets to "get by"—computers, the Internet, space shuttles! But once-upon-a-time in the Buckeye State, the "necessities" of life were quite different. Take a look! Do you know what all this stuff is?

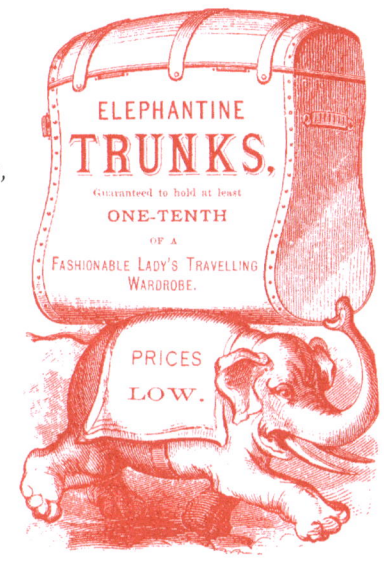

To Use. **The Necessary House:** This outdoor bathroom could be as plain as a shack with a hole in a bench, or as fancy as a fireplace-heated multi-holer (some cut small for kids!), with room for you and your friends!

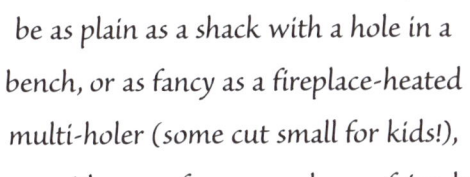

- **Out-Houses:** Today, we would call these outbuildings, barns, or stables. They were where the coach, harnesses for horses, farm equipment, ploughs and harrows, horses and other livestock, such as cows, pigs, sheep, and their feed supplies of hay, corn and oats were kept.

- **Smoke House:** This building was used for storage and to "cure" or preserve meat such as bacon, fish, etc.

- **Salt House:** Meat and fish were preserved by covering them with salt, usually in a wooden box or barrel.

- **Kitchen Larder:** Food supplies such as barrels of pickled tripe, whole salmon, jars of mangoes, pickled anchovies, and ropes of onions were stored in the larder.

- **Cook's Cellar:** This was a storage area partly underground where foods such as berries, vinegar, currants, brown sugar, rice, and lard were stored.

- **Scullery:** Laundry was done in this room in large wash tubs and iron pots on a "spit" over a fire. Coffee and chestnuts were roasted and candles were molded.

BASEBALL'S OPENING DAY

Cincinnati is home to Major League Baseball's oldest team—the Cincinnati Reds. The team was first named the Cincinnati Red Stockings when it was established way back in 1869. But unless you're from Cincinnati, you might not know about the special recognition of the city's rich baseball heritage. An ordinary day in many other baseball towns, Opening Day is very special in the hearts and minds of Cincinnati Reds fans. This rich tradition and respect for Opening Day goes back more than 100 years.

Starting in the 1890s, the Reds' business manager, Frank Bancroft, began promoting Opening Day as a very special day by organizing small parades and promoting the day as an event. The team began selling out the ballpark every Opening Day. Ever since those early days of baseball, Opening Day has been a very special one.

Marge Schott was one of the most beloved and most controversial figures in Cincinnati baseball history. Many of Schott's best moments came on Opening Day, which—along with the Findlay Market Parade—she cherished because of the unique place in Cincinnati's baseball history. Schott once was asked why she made such a big deal out of Opening Day. "Because of the fans, honey," she said. "I knew what separated us from everybody else. We had the first team, and we have the parade. We are the only one with a parade. I think Opening Day and the Findlay Market Parade are the two big things in Cincinnati. They go together!" Schott called Opening Day her "favorite day."

Greg Rhodes, executive director of the Reds Museum and Hall of Fame, believes that preserving the team's history is important. That's why he's written a book called Opening Day all about Cincinnati's special tradition. Rhodes described the Opening Day in this way: "Kids can get out of school; work closes down.... It doesn't say it on the calendar, but everybody in town knows that Opening Day is just different from every other day. It's a holiday in Cincinnati—there's no other place that's got that."

Cincinnati Reds, 1910

FRANK C. BANCROFT
Manager Cincinnati Club

Cincinnati Reds Statistics

Founded: 1865
Significance to U.S.: Oldest baseball franchise
Significance to Cincinnati: Largest sports organization
Plays: Cinergy Field
Annual Attendance: 2.4 million

Johnny Appleseed

John Chapman was born in Massachusetts in 1774. He had ten brothers and sisters. John's mother died when he was two and his father fought in the Revolutionary War. Johnny grew up near an apple orchard and enjoyed apples in many different kinds of food. When Ohio began to be settled, John decided to plant apple trees for the new settlements. With a sack of apple seeds, he canoed and walked all the way to Ohio. He would find places to plant without chopping down any trees because he did not want to harm nature in any way. He put the seeds in the ground and built a fence out of brush around the seeds. As the seeds began to grow into saplings, John cared for them. He sold his trees cheap, for a few pennies, because most of the pioneers did not have much money. Sometimes he gave away his seeds and saplings. It is said that "Johnny Appleseed," the nickname he was given, would walk around barefoot. He always carried a cooking pot and a bag of apple seeds. Johnny did not hunt animals for food, and he did not carry a knife or a gun either. He was a great storyteller and could always entertain new friends with his tales. Johnny planted apple trees in at least 15 counties in Ohio and then moved west to Indiana and Illinois. Johnny Appleseed was a great man because his apple trees helped the Ohioans survive. Johnny died after planting seeds for over 40 years.

Johnny's Apple Crisp

- 4-6 sliced apples
- 1/2 c. brown sugar
- 1 c. rolled oats
- 1 tsp. cinnamon
- 1/3 c. flour
- 1/4 c. butter
- 1/4 tsp. nutmeg

Place apples in buttered shallow baking dish. In a small bowl, mix all remaining ingredients until crumbly. Spread mixture over apples. Bake at 350 degrees for 40-45 minutes or until fruit is tender.

48 The OHIO Experience

OHIO FESTIVALS

Summer and fall festivals are very popular in Ohio. This is the time of year when people line the streets to watch parades, stuff themselves with festival food, and just have a good time. Ohio has many festivals to choose from, so you'd better mark your calendar to be sure you get a chance to go to your favorite ones!

Festival	When • Where
Algonquin Mill Fall Festival	*October • Carrollton, Ohio*
American Soya Festival	*September • Amanda, Ohio*
Ashtabula County Covered Bridge Festival	*October • Jefferson, Ohio*
Ashville 4th of July Celebration	*July • Ashville, Ohio*
Barnesville Pumpkin Festival	*September • Barnesville, Ohio*
Berea Grindstone Festival	*July • Berea, Ohio*
Brunswick Old Fashioned Days	*June • Brunswick, Ohio*
Bucyrus Bratwurst Festival	*August • Bucyrus, Ohio*
Circleville Pumpkin Show	*October • Circleville, Ohio*
Commercial Point Homecoming	*June • Commercial Point, Ohio*
Crestline Harvest-Antique Festival	*September • Crestline, Ohio*
Dalton Holidays Festival	*December • Dalton, Ohio*
Deercreek Dam Days Festival	*June • Williamsport, Ohio*
Dennison Railroad Festival	*May • Dennison, Ohio*
Fall Festival of Leaves	*October • Bainbridge, Ohio*
Feast of the Flowering Moon	*May • Chillicothe, Ohio*
Festival of the Fish	*June • Vermilion, Ohio*
First Town Days Festival	*July • New Philadelphia, Ohio*
Gallipolis River Recreation Festival	*July • Gallipolis, Ohio*
Geauga County Maple Festival	*April • Chardon, Ohio*
Geneva Area Grape Jamboree	*September • Geneva, Ohio*
Germantown Pretzel Festival	*September • Germantown, Ohio*
Holmes County Antique Festival	*October • Millersburg, Ohio*
Jackson Co. Apple Festival	*September • Jackson, Ohio*
Lancaster Old Car Club Spring Festival	*June • Lancaster, Ohio*
London Strawberry Festival	*June • London, Ohio*
Lorain International Festival	*June • Lorain, Ohio*
Mantua Potato Festival	*September • Mantua, Ohio*
Marion Popcorn Festival	*September • Marion, Ohio*
Miami Valley Steam Threshers Association	*July • Plain City, Ohio*
Milan Melon Festival	*September • Milan, Ohio*
Moonshine Festival	*May • New Straitsville, Ohio*
North Ridgeville Corn Festival	*August • North Ridgeville, Ohio*
Norwalk Jaycees Strawberry Festival	*May • Norwalk, Ohio, Ohio*

Oak Harbor Apple Festival	October • Oak Harbor, Ohio
Oak Hill Village Festival of Flags	May • Oak Hill, Ohio
Obetz Zucchinifest	August • Obetz, Ohio
Ohio Gourd Show	October • Mount Gilead, Ohio
Ohio Hills Folk Festival	July • Quaker City, Ohio
Ohio Swiss Festival, Inc.	October • Sugarcreek, Ohio
Ohio Tobacco Festival	August • Ripley, Ohio
Ohio Valley Antique Machinery Show	August • Georgetown, Ohio
Pemberville Free Fair	August • Pemberville, Ohio
Port Clinton Walleye Festival	May • Port Clinton, Ohio
Portsmouth River Days	September • Portsmouth, Ohio
Sweet Corn Festival, Inc.	September • Millersport, Ohio
The Baltimore Festival	August • Baltimore, Ohio
The Parade of the Hills	August • Nelsonville, Ohio
Tuscarawas County Italian-American Festival	August • New Philadelphia, Ohio
Utica Old Fashioned Ice Cream Festival	May • Utica, Ohio
Wellston Coal Festival	September • Wellston, Ohio
West Jefferson Annual Ox Roast	September • West Jefferson, Ohio
Wild Turkey Festival	May • McArthur, Ohio

To learn more about Ohio festivals, please contact:

Ohio Festivals & Events Association
2055 Cherokee Drive
London, Ohio 43140

On the Web at: http://www.ofea.org/

TALLSTACKS

The Tallstacks Music Arts and Heritage Festival was first held in 1988 in Cincinnati. Although the event is not an annual event, it is a well-known and popular festival celebrating riverboat heritage. Crowds of more than 500,000 people have been drawn to the event to see as many as 14 riverboats from as many as 10 states. Tall Stacks launched a legacy of pride in Cincinnati's rich river history and rekindled the nation's love affair with the steamboat.

To learn more about the Tallstacks Festival please contact:

Greater Cincinnati Tall Stacks Commission, Inc.
One West Fourth Street
Suite 512
Cincinnati, Ohio 45202

OHIO'S AMISH CULTURE

The world's largest Old Order Amish community, some 35,000 Ohioans, lives mostly in Defiance, Geauga, Holmes, Stark, Tuscarawas, and Wayne counties. The Amish live simple lives and do not use automobiles or electricity. The Amish base their everyday lives on many passages from the Bible.

Amish Dress Code ❖

Amish women do not cut their hair and at a very young age begin to wear it up. Women and girls wear a prayer covering most or all of the time. For housework or other chores, they may replace it with a kerchief in order not to mess up their usual prayer covering. Unmarried girls wear a black covering to church starting from the time they are teenagers. Married women generally wear white caps.

Like the women, Amish men wear their hair in simple fashions, most often in a bowl cut. Amish men wear hats most of the time. A hat would never be worn in church and most of the time they would remove their hats before going indoors. Little boys are often seen outdoors without hats more than men are, but boys wear the same type of hat as their fathers. In the summer, most men wear straw hats for working outside. For formal occasions, Amish men wear black felt hats.

Amish Weddings ❖

In some ways, Amish weddings are a throwback to the time when our great-grandparents got married. An Amish bride's dress is handmade, either by her or a close relative or friend. Her dress is most often a dark color and is not much different from her other dresses. Accompanied by a white cap and an apron, her wedding attire will become her "Sunday best" after she is married. The groom wears a new black suit, which will also serve the same purpose for him. Normally, Amish men do not wear ties, but for the occasion they will wear bow ties.

Amish weddings generally take place at the home of the bride's parents, in a barn, or in another building large enough to hold all of the wedding guests. Many wedding ceremonies are held in the morning. As in church services, the men and women do not sit together, but they face each other, including the bridal party. Other differences are found in the length of the service itself. Amish wedding ceremonies often last three hours with all of the clergymen offering a sermon, usually starting with the first book of the Bible and continuing through the entire Bible.

For the vows, the couple and their witnesses face the preacher. The entire congregation rises to show their support of the couple. The groom and bride repeat the traditional vows, but Amish couples do not exchange wedding rings. Amish people do not wear any kind of jewelry.

The biggest part of an Amish wedding is all of the work it takes to prepare the food. Amish cookbooks often include recipes for hundreds of people. Weddings are a huge event for the bride's entire family. Several days before the ceremony, women of the community come to clean the house, move furniture, and begin cooking. The bride and groom ask friends and relatives to be cooks and servers on their big day. This is an honor, and the helpers, arriving before sunrise, commit themselves to an entire day of work. A typical Amish wedding meal consists of chicken, bread dressing, mashed potatoes and gravy, noodles, salads, fruits, pies, and date pudding.

Amish couples do not go on a honeymoon, but instead stay at the bride's parents' house to help put everything back in order. Amish wedding showers often take place after the wedding. The couple usually receives items such as dishes, cookware, and canned food.

COVERED BRIDGES

◆ There were once more than 12,000 covered bridges in the United States, most of them east of the Mississippi. A total of approximately 3,500, or more than a quarter of all U.S. bridges, were built in Ohio. This makes sense if you think about the number of rivers and streams in Ohio! ◆ In the 1800s, several designs for the truss or support system were patented. Truss bridges were a series of repeated triangles, some of which were reinforced with steel rods. Trusses let builders create bridges as long as 200 feet or more. No two bridges were exactly alike because each individual river or stream brought its own touches that had to be considered. The bridges were covered to protect the trusses from the weather. An uncovered wooden bridge could last 20 years, while covered ones can last for a century or more. ◆ Each fall Ashtabula County in northeast Ohio hosts an annual Covered-Bridge Festival. Ashtabula County is home to 16 covered bridges. Today there are still more than 160 covered bridges in Ohio.

The OHIO Experience

WORLD'S LARGEST IN OHIO

World's Largest Rubber-Stamp
Cleveland, Ohio

In 1985, the Amoco Oil Company commissioned artist Claes Oldenburg to create the 28-foot-tall stamp, intended for the lobby of the company's headquarters. Before the stamp was finished, the company had a change in management and the new boss did not care much for the huge rubber stamp with the word "FREE" on it. The stamp was then put in storage in a warehouse in Indiana. Finally, another company executive questioned why Amoco was paying the storage fee on a huge rubber stamp. In 1991, Amoco offered to donate the stamp to Cleveland as a piece of public art. The city complained that they did not have the funds to install or maintain it. Amoco offered to do the job for "FREE" and now it sits near the harbor in downtown Cleveland.

World's Largest Field of Corn
Dublin, Ohio

Title: Field of Corn (with Osage Orange Trees)
Material: Concrete
Height of Ears: 6 feet
Number of Ears: 109

Dublin, Ohio's Sam and Eulalia Frantz Park is located on the corner of Rings and Frantz Roads. More than 100 concrete ears of corn rise up 5–6 feet from the ground. Created in 1994, the commissioned art by Malcolm Cochran symbolizes a celebration of Dublin's history as a farming community and serves as a memorial to rural landscape being consumed by urban development. Sam Frantz, a pioneer in corn hybridization, once owned the site of the cornfield.

World's Largest Cuckoo Clock
Wilmot, Ohio

Length: 13 feet 6 inches
Width: 24 feet
Height: 23 feet 6 inches

The world's largest cuckoo clock is located at Alpine-Alpa, a Swiss restaurant in Ohio's Amish country. The figures come to life when the clock strikes the hour and a wooden band plays while wooden dancers with braids twirl around.

OHIO TRIVIA!

Birthplace of Aluminum • Charles M. Hall can be thanked for a world full of aluminum siding and aluminum everything else. Hall would do experiments to find a cheap way to make aluminum in an old woodshed while he was still in high school. He attended Oberlin College, where he continued to experiment. Eight months after graduating, at the age of twenty-two, Hall discovered the process he and many others had been seeking. After a patent dispute with a French scientist, Hall borrowed money from Andrew Mellon and built what became the American Aluminum Company.

First Mormon Temple • The first Mormon Temple in the United States was not in Utah; it was built in Kirtland Hills, Ohio. Prophet Joseph Smith and his followers, including Brigham Young, constructed the temple in 1833. The establishment brought many new people to town. Financial problems, including the failure of the church bank, caused Smith and Young to flee Ohio.

Salt Creek • Long before settlers discovered what is now Jackson County, Native Americans came to Salt Creek for its salt. The first pioneers to take advantage of the creek did so in 1798. They would draw water from 30-foot wells and would boil it in huge kettles. Due to the low salinity of the water, up to fifteen gallons of water were required to produce one pound of salt. The discovery of other saltworks both more accessible and with higher salinity led to the decline of Salt Creek's commercial value.
(salinity: the amount of salt in the water)

America's First Concrete Street

Once a Native American settlement, Bellefontaine, Ohio is most famous for something we take for granted today—paved roads. It was there in 1891 that the Buckeye Cement Company laid an 8-foot strip of concrete on Main Street—America's first concrete street. The company later paved around the courthouse, which brought engineers from across the country. A section of the street was displayed at the 1893 Chicago World's Fair, winning a gold medal.

Grand Lake St. Mary's

Stretching from Lake Erie to the Ohio River, the construction of the Miami and Erie Canal was a major development in the state. For the canal to succeed, it needed a reliable water source at its high point. About 1,700 men, paid 30 cents a day, labored for years to create Grand Lake St. Mary's, the largest man-made lake in the world when it was completed in 1845.

Keene's Fireproof House

Fred Sharby was afraid of fire. Two of the theaters he owned burned flat, and he was terrified of dying in a fire. As a result, he tore down his house on the north side of Roxbury Street in Keene, Ohio and built a new one of all fireproof materials. Steel girders, stucco, plaster, fireproof floor tiles, doors of solid metal, and a furnace enclosed in cement walls have indeed lasted to this day without a fire. Fred, unfortunately, was not so lucky. He chose the night of November 28, 1942, to go to the Cocoanut Grove in Boston, Massachusetts and died in one of the country's worst fires—492 people were killed!

INTERESTING FACTS ABOUT OHIO!

INTENSE EXCITEMENT!

The OHIO Experience

About the Authors...

Carole Marsh has been writing about Ohio and the United States for more than 20 years. The Georgia native is the creator of more than 15,000 products, primarily fiction and non-fiction supplementary educational materials including books, interactive CD-ROMs, games, and online adventures. These products include *proven* comprehensive state curriculum products for Virginia, Georgia, Wisconsin, Illinois, and now Ohio, too! These curriculum series have yielded outstanding results—sometimes raising test scores by as much as 400%! In addition, Carole is the founder and CEO of Gallopade International and the founder and owner of Marsh Media, a public relations and corporate communications firm. Carole Marsh's works and accomplishments have been celebrated for years. She is the recipient of the 2004 Teachers' Choice℠ Award for the Family by *Learning® Magazine*, the winner of the 2003 Excellence in Education Award from the National School Supply and Equipment Association and Advance America 2002 Award of Excellence.

Chad Beard, a Michigan native, loves researching the history of Ohio and its people. Chad enjoys genealogy, history, and music. "The Ohio Experience gave me an excuse to do more research on Ohio." Chad explained, "My family tree has many roots that lead back to Hancock County, Ohio."

Rachel Moss is a senior at Sandy Creek High School in Tyrone, Georgia. Rachel has always had a love for reading and as a result has a gift for research and writing.

Steven St. Laurent, a native Rhode Islander, has enjoyed writing since elementary school—he's ghost-written two novels. He enjoys his family time, home improvement and letterboxing.